Tilly
and the DRAGON

HILARY McKAY

AW

For Marie and Lillie Williams,
with love.
H.M.

To my little Sister Sophie.
I love you kid x
M.S.

EGMONT

We bring stories to life

Book Band: Gold

This edition first published in Great Britain 2014
by Egmont UK Ltd, The Yellow Building,
1 Nicholas Road, London W11 4AN.
Text copyright © Hilary McKay 2014
Illustrations copyright © Mick Shaw 2014
Art direction by Kimberley Scott
The author and illustrator have asserted their moral rights.
ISBN 978 1 4052 67212
10 9 8 7 6 5 4 3 2 1
A CIP catalogue record for this title is available from the British Library.
Printed in Singapore.
55194/1
www.egmont.co.uk

EGMONT LUCKY COIN

Our story began over a century ago, when seventeen-year-old
Egmont Harald Petersen found a coin in the street.

He was on his way to buy a flyswatter, a small hand-operated
printing machine that he then set up in his tiny apartment.

The coin brought him such good luck that today Egmont has
offices in over 30 countries around the world. And that lucky
coin is still kept at the company's head offices in Denmark.

Mum & Dad

Timmy

♥ Polar ♥

Granny

Uncle Kevin

Great Uncle Max

Tilly (me!)

The Rough Lot

by Tilly

CONTENTS

How Tilly Made the Toast   5

The Dragon in the Bedroom   12

The Dragon and the Bath   20

The Moat and the Rough Lot   26

The Magic Word   39

Red Bananas

HOW TILLY MADE
THE TOAST

In Tilly's house there lived:

Tilly's father, Tilly's mother.

Tilly's little brother Timmy.

Tilly's dog. His name was Polar.

Tilly, and the dragon.

The dragon was in Tilly's bedroom.
He had been there for a week.

He was a nice dragon, very dark green,
with golden eyes and red wings and a red
line of pointy bits all along his back.

'He's a perfect dragon,' said Tilly.

Tilly had found the dragon under a sad and
scary sign:

She had taken him home and given him a
lovely meal of logs and coal, with candles
for pudding.

Afterwards he had fallen asleep in her bedroom. And there he had stayed.

At first only Timmy and Tilly knew he was there.

'Tilly,' asked Timmy, 'is that dragon safe?'

'Perfectly safe,' said Tilly. 'Don't worry, Timmy! There's nothing in my bedroom that could hurt him, and even if he fell out of the window, he could fly.'

'Oh,' said Timmy. 'Did Mummy say you could have a dragon in your bedroom?'

'No,' said Tilly.

'Did Daddy?'

'No,' said Tilly.

'Did anyone?'

'No one said I couldn't,' said Tilly.

Tilly's parents only found out about the dragon when the toaster broke.

'Never mind,' said Tilly, picking up Timmy's untoasted toast. 'I'll put it on the dragon.'

'Put it on the what?' asked Tilly's mother.

'Dragon,' said Tilly, disappearing.

'Dragon!' said Tilly's father. 'Did she say dragon? Not possible!'

'I've been telling you for ages that Tilly has a dragon in her bedroom!' said Timmy.

'Have you? Have you?' asked his mother, and she went hurrying out of the kitchen just as Tilly came back with the toast.

'Nice and hot and crunchy,' Tilly said cheerfully to Timmy. 'Jam or Marmite?'

'Jam on one side,' ordered Timmy. 'Marmite on the other. Butter on both.'

'I think you should say "please,"' said Tilly, jamming and buttering.

'Do you?' asked Timmy.

'Yes, and I think you should say "thank you,"' said Tilly, Marmiting.

Timmy reached for his toast and took such a large bite that he couldn't say anything. Then their mother came rushing back and said, 'Tilly! There's a DRAGON in your BEDROOM!'

'Completely impossible,' said Tilly's father.

'Perfectly possible,' said Tilly. 'That's how I made the toast.'

THE DRAGON IN THE BEDROOM

Tilly's parents often worried about the things in Tilly's bedroom. The crumby plates and sticky mugs. The scooter she was mending. The wellies, the paint pots and the layers of paper and socks. Now they worried about the dragon.

'Tilly!' they said. 'You CAN'T keep a dragon in your bedroom!'

But Tilly could.

'He makes the floor look tidier,' she said.
'Now it isn't covered in lots of things. It's just
covered in one thing. Dragon. It's really not a
problem. He's always careful to smoke out of
the window.'

'Smoke out of the window?' asked her
worried parents.

'Yes,' said Tilly. 'He's very polite.'

The dragon filled Tilly's bedroom. Now a hot toasted carpet smell woke her in the mornings and she had to climb a scaly dragon mountain to get into bed at night. She didn't mind. She was perfectly happy.

Tilly's family were not happy.

Timmy didn't like going near at all. He walked sideways with his round blue eyes on the door.

When he reached his own bedroom he rushed in very quickly and banged it shut.

'Not very friendly,' said Tilly.

Eek!

Tilly's mother and father stopped going up the stairs completely. They reached their bedroom by a ladder to the window. They swung across to the bathroom by ropes. They climbed right over the roof and down the other side to tuck up Timmy at night.

They were not polite to the dragon.

'Don't talk about scorching underneath his window!' begged Tilly. 'Don't send Timmy to bed with buckets of water! Don't keep sneezing and saying it's the smoke! I'm sure he notices.'

Tilly was kind. She borrowed the newspaper and read him all the warm weather forecasts and other hot news.

HOT GOSSIP

But Tilly's father brought home a fire engine
and parked it in the garden.

'A FIRE ENGINE!' said Timmy, and
switched on the siren.

The noise was awful. Tilly rushed upstairs and
found the poor dragon pale with shock. Lime-
green and pink, instead of dark green and red.

18

The garden filled with puddles as Timmy turned on the hose. Water splashed hard against the window. The dragon dived under the bed and Tilly said, 'Dragon, I think we need to find you a more peaceful home.'

The dragon nodded, and so did the bed that he was wearing as a hat.

'I'll fetch my wheelbarrow so you won't get wet in the puddles,' said Tilly. 'You can have a nice ride and you needn't get out until we find somewhere perfect.'

THE DRAGON AND
THE BATH

The dragon held on tight as Tilly bumped him down the stairs and through the front door, and across the splashy garden.

'I think,' said Tilly, 'I shall take you to see my dear old Granny. Her house has very hot central heating. And it's all pink. Even the bath in the bathroom is pink!'

The dragon suddenly clutched the front of the wheelbarrow. Tilly didn't notice because she was working so hard, pushing.

She was glad when they arrived and found
Granny in her garden.

'Hullo Tilly!' called Granny, waving. 'Now what have you got in that wheelbarrow? Is it for me?'

'Yes it is!' said Tilly, hugging Granny. 'Dragon, this is my dear old Granny! Granny, this is my favourite dragon! He's come to live with you!'

The dragon shyly held out a huge taloned foot to shake hands with Granny.

Granny screamed and ran into the house.

'Did you see those nails?' she cried to Tilly (who ran after her). 'Black as black!'

'He's a dragon!' said Tilly, laughing. 'Of course they're black as black!'

'And the state of his knees!' said Granny, grabbing scrubbing brushes and soap. 'Bright green! But don't worry! Leave him with me, Tilly dear, or you'll be late for lunch.'

So Tilly left the dragon with Granny and she tried not to worry. But when she rushed back afterwards the wheelbarrow had gone. She found it in the bathroom. The dragon was still inside, carefully not looking at Granny.

'He just won't move!' Granny told Tilly. 'Not for a nice hot bath! Not to have his knees washed! Not even to have his nails scrubbed, although they are black as black.'

'The thing is, Granny,' said Tilly, 'I don't think dragons enjoy baths.'

'He doesn't have to enjoy it!' said Granny. 'He just has to get into it!'

But Tilly didn't agree with that, and so she picked up the handles of the wheelbarrow once again.

THE MOAT AND THE ROUGH LOT

'We'll go to Uncle Kevin's house,' Tilly told the dragon. 'You'll like it! There are dungeons and drawbridges and battlements and ballrooms. The chimneys are enormous but I've never seen a bathroom!'

Uncle Kevin was busy polishing his cannons when Tilly and the dragon arrived.

'Golly gosh, what have you got there?' he asked, staring at the wheelbarrow.

'It's a dragon,' said Tilly. 'For you! Please look after it very carefully because it's a very special one!'

'It's a beauty!' said Uncle Kevin. 'Where shall we put it? On the roof between the turrets? Whatever is it made of? It looks just like real!'

'It is real!' said Tilly.

'Nonsense, Tilly!' said Uncle Kevin. 'It's a very clever copy!'

And he gave the dragon a good prod on the nose to prove he was right.

'OUCH!' he yelled a moment later, blowing on his burnt fingers. 'It's hot! What are you thinking of, Tilly? I can't put a thing like that on the roof! But don't worry Tilly! Leave it with me while you go for your tea, and I will think of something.'

So Tilly left the dragon with Uncle Kevin, but she could not help worrying and as soon she could she rushed back.

The dragon was still in the wheelbarrow, and now there was a large notice beside him.

ROLL UP!
ROLL UP!

SEE THE

DRAGON
DIVE!

THREE STICKS:
FIFTY PENCE

PLEASE KEEP SMALL
CHILDREN AWAY FROM
THE EDGE THE MOAT

There was a long line of people waiting. Uncle Kevin was at the front, collecting money in a hat and giving out bundles of sticks. He looked wet but cheerful.

'You're just in time!' he told Tilly. 'I've turned it into a tourist attraction! Watch!'

31

The little boy at the front of the line flung a stick into the water.

'And . . . FETCH!' shouted Uncle Kevin to the dragon.

The dragon held on terribly tight and closed his eyes.

'It's not going to do it,' said the little boy.

'Little boy, you're not being helpful,' said Uncle Kevin. 'FETCH! GOOD DRAGON! FETCH!'

'You'll never get that dragon out of that wheelbarrow,' said the little boy. 'And what about my stick?'

'Oh, really, not again!' growled Uncle Kevin, raised his arms above his head, dived like a seagull into the moat, grabbed the stick, climbed out and bowed to the cheering watchers.

'He's done that eleven times now!' said the little boy to Tilly. 'Only once we've had to drag him out. I'm buying more sticks!'

Tilly looked around. The crowd seemed perfectly happy to pay to watch Uncle Kevin dive. The tourist attraction didn't need a dragon at all. Very quietly she picked up the handles of the wheelbarrow and slipped away.

'We'll try the Rough Lot,' she said to the dragon.

The Rough Lot were the part of Tilly's family that lived on the other side of town. They had lots of dogs and children, a small messy house and a large messy garden. They were very fond of Tilly and she was very fond of them. She told the Rough Lot father all her problems.

The Rough Lot father scratched his head. 'One thing to get hold of a dragon, Till,' he said. 'Quite another to get rid of it. Never mind. You get home now, before you're late for bed. Leave it with me and I'll have a think.'

Tilly left the dragon quite happily with the Rough Lot. She knew, however rough they were, they were very kind to animals. *Perhaps the dragon will get out of the wheelbarrow there,* she thought hopefully.

But the dragon didn't. Not when the Rough Lot mother brought him a splashy cup of tea.

Not when the Rough Lot father wheeled him to the pub.

Not when the big boys lifted the damp sticky toddlers up to pat him.

Not when the friendly dogs licked his face.

In the morning, when Tilly came running back, the dragon was exactly where she had left him.

'There's ways of shifting donkeys with carrots,' said the Rough Lot father. 'And there's ways of shifting sheep with dogs. There's ways of shifting elephants with buns, but I don't know any way of shifting a dragon except for a hosepipe.'

'No thank you!' said Tilly.

'Then,' said the Rough Lot father, 'that dragon's stuck in that wheelbarrow for life!'

'All this dragon wants,' said Tilly sadly as she wheeled the dragon away, 'is a polite, dry home where everyone loves him.'

'Don't we all?' said the Rough Lot father.

THE MAGIC WORD

'There's only one person left,' Tilly told the dragon as she plodded slowly along. 'And that's Great Uncle Max, and the whole family say he is bonkers. But at least he has beautiful . . .'

Tilly stopped so suddenly that the wheelbarrow nearly fell over. They had arrived, but Great Uncle Max's house was gone. It had vanished under a great heap of purple and yellow stripes. Tangled amongst the stripes were ropes. In the middle of the stripes and ropes was Great Uncle Max. He was in a flap.

40

'Dear oh dear oh DEAR!' he was murmuring. 'Calamity, calamity, CALAMITY. Oh the absolute UNBEARABLENESS of damp matches!'

The dragon suddenly gave a snort of agreement. Great Uncle Max looked up.

'Oh!' he exclaimed. 'What a WONDERFUL surprise! My dear fellow! (And you of course too, Tilly!) How, very, very, nice!'

'. . . manners!' Tilly murmured to the dragon. 'He has beautiful manners! That's what I was going to say.'

The dragon nodded, and looked thoughtfully at Great Uncle Max.

'I'm in rather a pickle,' said Great Uncle Max. 'The flame went out and we came down very suddenly and now the matches won't light!'

'Oh, it's your hot air balloon!' exclaimed Tilly, suddenly understanding the purple and yellow stripes.

'Yes, but without any hot air,' said Great Uncle Max unhappily.

'So is it stuck?'

'It couldn't be stucker,' said Great Uncle Max.

'We could help,' suggested Tilly. 'I could untangle the ropes and if the dragon would get out of the wheelbarrow he could . . . perhaps . . . stand in the middle . . . and blow . . .'

'Blow what?' asked Great Uncle Max.

'Hot air!' said Tilly.

'Why, that would be wonderful!' said Great Uncle Max. 'My dear dragon! *Please*!'

Then at last, the dragon climbed out of the wheelbarrow.

And blew.

Then the purple-and-yellow-striped
landscape turned into a purple-and-yellow-
striped hot air balloon.

And Great Uncle Max said to the dragon,
'I suppose you wouldn't care for a tour of the
Active Volcanoes of the South?'

And the dragon glowed with pleasure.

After she had waved goodbye, Tilly went home with her empty wheelbarrow.

Every single person she met asked the same question:

'How ever did you get him out?'

'It was Great Uncle Max,' explained Tilly. 'Not me.'

'But what did he do?'

'He didn't do anything,' said Tilly, 'He just said, "Please!"'

'Please?'

'Yes.'

'Was that the magic word?'

'Yes.'

'Crikey!' said the Rough Lot.

'Golly gosh!' said Uncle Kevin.

'Good gracious!' said dear old Granny.

'Well done!' said Tilly's father and mother when they tucked Tilly up in bed that night. 'One little word! Amazing!'

'It wasn't amazing at all,' said Tilly sleepily. 'I told you from the beginning: dragons are very polite!'

by Tilly